ALI THE GREAT

and the Dinosaur Mistake

by SAADIA FARUQI   illustrated by DEBBY RAHMALIA

raintree 🌱

a Capstone company — publishers for children

FoR AdaM —SF
FoR ALesha —DR

Raintree is an imprint of Capstone Global Library Limited, a company
incorporated in England and Wales having its registered office at 264
Banbury Road, Oxford, OX2 7DY – Registered company number: 6695582

www.raintree.co.uk
myorders@raintree.co.uk

Text © Capstone Global Library Limited 2024
The moral rights of the proprietor have been asserted.

All rights reserved. No part of this publication may be reproduced in
any form or by any means (including photocopying or storing it in
any medium by electronic means and whether or not transiently or
incidentally to some other use of this publication) without the written
permission of the copyright owner, except in accordance with the
provisions of the Copyright, Designs and Patents Act 1988 or under the
terms of a licence issued by the Copyright Licensing Agency, 5th Floor,
Shackleton House, 4 Battle Bridge Lane, London SE1 2HX (www.cla.
co.uk). Applications for the copyright owner's written permission should
be addressed to the publisher.

Designed by Kay Fraser and Tracy Davies
Original illustrations © Capstone Global Library Limited 2024
Originated by Capstone Global Library Ltd

978 1 3982 5298 1

British Library Cataloguing in Publication Data
A full catalogue record for this book is available from the British Library.

Printed and bound in India.

CONTENTS

I'm Ali Tahir, also known as

ALI THE GREAT!

And this is my family...

ABBA
doctor

AMMA
scientist

DADA
chief joke teller

DADI
best cook in
the world

FATEH
sneaky little brother

LET'S LEARN SOME URDU!

Ali and his family speak both English and Urdu, a language from Pakistan. Now you'll know some Urdu too!

ABBA (also baba) father

AMMA (also mama) mother

BHAI brother

DADA grandfather on father's side

DADI grandmother on father's side

SALAAM hello

SHUKRIYA thank you

Chapter 1

THE MUSEUM

Today was a very special day. Ms Alex's class was at the museum. It was a big, shiny building with gardens all around.

"This is so cool!" Ali said as he climbed off the bus.

"I love museums," Yasmin said.
"We can learn all sorts of things
here!"

Ali grinned. "Too late for me. I
already know everything."

Yasmin laughed.

Ms Alex made them all stand in
a line. "You must be on your best
behaviour!" she told them.

"We will!" Emma replied, smiling.

A volunteer met them at the entrance. "I'm Taylor," he said. "Please make sure you follow museum rules at all times."

"Rules?" Ali whispered. He thought rules were boring. He liked doing things his way.

"No running or jumping. No eating or drinking. No touching the exhibits," Taylor said.

"Especially the dinosaurs."

Ali's eyes grew wide. "I love
dinosaurs!" he cried. "I know all
about them!"

Chapter 2

PALAEONTOLOGY

Taylor showed the children around. They saw mummies from ancient Egypt. "So creepy!" Zack said.

Then they saw minerals and gems. "So beautiful," Emma said.

They spent a long time
reading facts about the human
body.

"Did you know we have 206
bones in our body?" Yasmin
asked.

"Yes, I know that!" Ali said impatiently. "But where are the dinosaurs?"

Finally, Taylor led them to the palaeontology exhibit.

Ali looked around with his mouth open. Huge dinosaur skeletons reached up to the ceiling. "Whoa!" he whispered.

"Pa-lae-on-to-lo-gy," Yasmin read from the sign.

"That means the study of dinosaurs," Ali told her. He'd read it in a book about dinosaurs that Abba had given him.

"Correct," Taylor replied. "Dinosaurs lived millions of years ago, before humans and most other animals."

Ali already knew that too.

"Look, a T. rex!" he shouted,

pointing to a huge dinosaur.

"Whoa!" Zack said.

Taylor held up his hand.

"Actually, that's an allosaurus."

"I thought you knew

everything," Zack teased Ali.

Ali shrugged. "It was just a mistake."

Taylor pointed to another big skeleton. "*That's* the T. rex," he said. "Do you know what it liked to eat?"

"Plants!" Ali said quickly. But wait, T. rex was the biggest, baddest dinosaur. Maybe Ali was wrong about the plants?

"T. rex ate other dinosaurs!" Zack shouted.

"Correct!" Taylor replied. "T. rex was a meat eater."

Ali scowled. He was supposed to be the dinosaur expert, not Zack!

Chapter 3

MISTAKES ARE OKAY

"Do you think there are any dinosaurs left in the world today?" Taylor asked the children.

Ali rolled his eyes. What a
silly question. He definitely knew
the answer to this one. "Of course
not. They're all extinct now."

Taylor shook his head. "Actually, birds are a type of dinosaur."

Ali looked at the floor. "Oh, yeah," he whispered. He was embarrassed about his mistakes. He wasn't an expert at all!

Taylor came over to him.

"Don't worry, buddy. It's okay to

get things wrong."

Ali looked up. "Really?"

"Yep," Taylor replied.
"Scientists often make mistakes.
But they learn from them and do
better next time."

Ali grinned. "Then I'm a
scientist for sure. My mistakes
are expert-level!"

JUST JOKING AROUND

What do you call a dinosaur that's sleeping?
A dino-snore

Why should you never ask a dinosaur to tell you a story?
Because their TALES are so long

What do you call a dinosaur that doesn't shower?
Stink-o-saurus

DINO FACTS!

- ☆ The first dinosaur bones were discovered in the 1800s.

- ☆ Some dinosaurs were very big, like the T. rex. But there were also many dinosaurs as small as chickens.

- ☆ Not all dinosaurs were meat eaters. Some ate plants.

- ☆ Dinosaurs became extinct more than 65 million years ago.

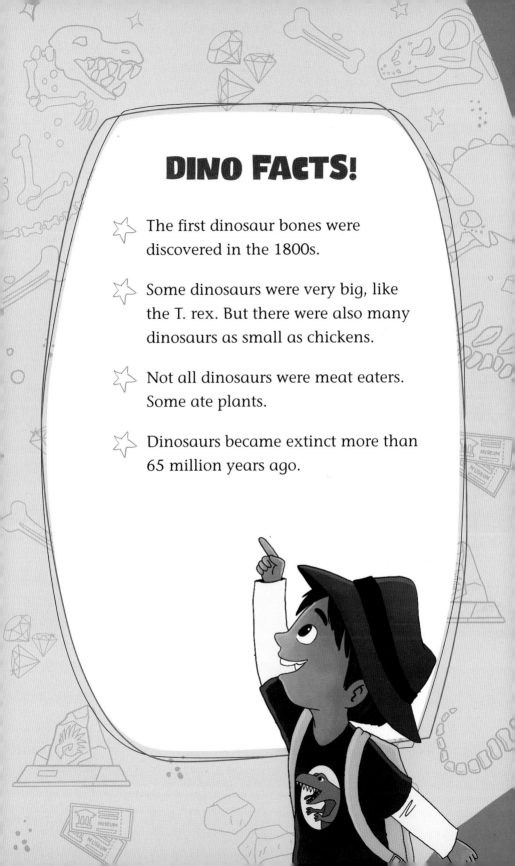

THINK **BIG** WITH

ALI THE GREAT!

☆ Think about a time that you made a mistake. How did you feel? Next time that happens, remind yourself that it's okay to make mistakes!

☆ Is there a topic that you consider yourself an "expert" in? Write five facts about a topic you know well and draw a picture to go with it.

☆ If you could go to any museum in the world, where would you go? Make a list of subjects you'd like to learn about and where you'd like to go to learn about them.

☆ About the authoR ☆

Saadia Faruqi is a Pakistani American writer, interfaith activist and cultural sensitivity trainer featured in *O, The Oprah Magazine*. Author of the Yasmin chapter book series, Saadia also writes other books for children, including *Yusuf Azeem Is Not a Hero*. Saadia is editor-in-chief of *Blue Minaret*, an online magazine of poetry, short stories and art. Besides writing, she also loves reading, binge-watching her favourite series, and taking naps.

☆ About the iLLustRatoR ☆

Debby Rahmalia is an illustrator based in Indonesia with a passion for storytelling. She enjoys creating diverse works that showcase an array of cultures and people. Debby's long-term dream was to become an illustrator. She was encouraged to pursue her dream after she had her first baby and has been illustrating ever since. When she's not drawing, she spends her time reading the books she illustrated to her daughter or wandering around the neighbourhood with her.

JOIN **ALI THE GREAT** on his adventures!

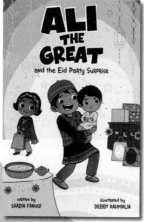